Nagini

Ron Weasley™

Lucius Malfoy's ring

Golden egg

Dark Mark 'tattoo'

Common Welsh
Green

Chinese
Fireball
dragon

Swedish Short-
Snout dragon

Hermione Granger™

Hungarian Horntail dragon

TM & © Warner Bros. Entertainment Inc. Harry Potter Publishing Rights © JKR. (s05)

HARRY AND THE
HUNGARIAN
HORNTAIL DRAGON

FAWKES™ THE
PHOENIX

Triwizard Cup

Goblet of Fire™

VIKTOR KRUM

HARRY POTTER™

FLEUR DELACOUR

CEDRIC DIGGORY

MERPERSON

Grindylow

HARRY POTTER